FIRE IN THE SKY

Written and illustrated by
Mick Manning and Brita Granström

Collins

By 1944, five years into World War II, Sergeant Norman Jackson had survived 30 missions over Germany ... but many of his friends had been killed.

2

One night, his plane was attacked by an enemy fighter. A fuel tank in the wing caught fire!

3

Jackson knew he had to put the fire out to save the lives of the crew. He climbed out of the escape hatch.

You're crazy!

We're doing 200 miles per hour!

Hold his parachute.

4

The fighter attacked again, blasting Jackson into the night sky.

With his parachute on fire, he fell 6,000 metres.

Aaghhh!

But Jackson fell on soft branches.

9

Badly burnt, with bullets in his leg, Jackson found help.

10

Four of your crewmates survived.

Jackson spent many months in hospital being treated by German doctors.

In 1945, Norman Jackson was awarded the Victoria Cross for his bravery.

Ideas for reading

Written by Gillian Howell
Primary Literacy Consultant

Learning objectives: *(reading objectives correspond with Blue band; all other objectives correspond with Diamond band)* use phonics to read unknown words; understand underlying themes, causes and points of view; use the technique of dialogic talk to explore ideas, topics or issues; select words and language drawing on their knowledge of literary features and formal and informal writing

Curriculum links: History: What are we remembering on Remembrance Day?

High frequency words: in, by, five, had, over, but, many, of, his, been, one, night, was, an, a, in, the, it, to, put, out, lives, he, on, with, him, off, I, must, with, my, you, four, your, for

Interest words: Sergeant, survived, missions, enemy fighter, escape hatch, parachute, crewmates, Victoria Cross

Resources: paper, pens, pencils

Word count: 189

Getting started

- Ask the children in pairs to think about something brave that their partner has done and explain why they think it was brave.

- Read the title together and look at the front cover. Encourage the children to share what they know about flying during World War II. Ask them what they think the crew of a plane would do if it caught fire.

- Ask the children to turn to the back cover and read the blurb. Explain that this is a graphic novel and discuss what features the book will have, flicking through and pointing out the multiple frames and speech bubbles. Explain that the story is told through the text and the frames of artwork, and discuss how the children will read this book.

Reading and responding

- Ask the children to read the book using a quiet voice. Remind them to use their phonic knowledge to work out new words and break longer words into syllables.

- On p2, discuss what a Sergeant is and check the children know how to read the word. If children have difficulty reading *missions*, explain that the *ss* sounds as *sh*.

- As they read, pause and ask the children to say what extra information about Jackson they get from reading the speech bubbles. For example, on p4, ask what the other crew thought about Jackson's actions.

- Ask the children to continue reading to the end of the book, listening to them as they read and praising them for attempting unfamiliar words.